For information regarding permission
write to Emma Howard Books
P.O.Box 385, Planetarium Station
New York, N.Y. 10024-0385

Published by Emma Howard Books
New York
Printed in the Philippines
by Paragon Printing Corporation

Library of Congress Catalogue Card Number: 99-94093
ISBN 1-886551-06-5

Jacket Illustration copyright Rachel Nickerson Luna 1999
Jacket Design Armando Luna

Darinka
The Little Artist Deer

Rachel Nickerson Luna

Emma Howard Books
New York

Darinka was a little deer. She lived in a
big forest with a herd of fluffy-tailed deer.
When the other deer were basking in the sunlight,
Darinka would search for patches of hard ground
where she could draw pictures.

The older deer eyed her with amusement. "There is
little Darinka, drawing again!" they would say to one
another.

Darinka wanted to use lots of colors in her pictures, but in the forest it was difficult to find colors to use. When the berries were ripe, she could gather blue and red berries to make into paint for her pictures on rocks and trees.

One day while she was looking for somewhere to draw, she heard two old bucks talking about a place called "New York City" where there were lots of artists and people who loved art. It was a big city made of brick and concrete away down the river. People thought it was a fabulous place, but the old bucks laughed to think of going there. "It's no place for a deer," said one. "That's right," said the other, "There are no soft meadows where we could lie in the warm sunlight."

Darinka's little ears tingled to hear about this city where artists lived. Surely she would be able to get paint of every color and meet other artists too.

She decided to make a raft and float down the river until she found this city. She gathered sticks and twigs. She tied them all together with green grape vines. She pushed her raft into the water and hopped on. Off she drifted, down the river.

The further she drifted from home, the more black and murky the water became. She imagined huge deer-eating sea monsters, giant clams, and ferocious octopi. She kept her little hooves on her raft and tried to keep her eyes looking down the river where she hoped the city would soon appear.

Carefully she steered out of the way of barges and tugboats. At last she saw New York City - so big and grand in the afternoon sun! Darinka had never seen anything like it. The little deer was so excited to see the place of her hopes and dreams.

She landed on the bank of the river at a place called Riverside Park. It had trees, grass, and flowers that reminded her of home. She made herself a fine nest of branches and leaves. She also found berries to eat. Then she decided to rest until the next day when she would explore the city and discover where the artists painted and displayed their work.

The next day Darinka realized that the old bucks were right. New York City was a city of cement and brick. She saw hardly a flower or tree outside her park. The buildings were taller than any tree she had ever seen, and the sidewalks were harder than the forest floor. The noise of the buses and the taxi horns hurt her ears!

She walked and walked until she reached a place where the buildings were not so tall. There were artists here, she could tell, because in every window she could see the colors of many paintings and on every building she saw a sign reading "Gallery." She looked all around and talked to gallery owners and artists. This was the heart of the city for the little artist deer.

Now she had to get busy. She needed art supplies, but how could she pay for them? In the forest everything was free.

She found an art supply store nearby. She was spellbound by all the colors she saw. Every color she could imagine was sealed up in a tube!

Darinka asked to see the manager and told him her predicament. He was sympathetic and allowed Darinka to open a charge account. He also arranged for her supplies to be delivered to Riverside Park. Darinka scampered home to begin painting scenes of deer and forests.

When she had finished about twenty paintings, she went to all her favorite galleries to tell the owners about her work. She described her wonderful paintings, but no one cared. No one wanted to see them. She became very sad and wished that she had never come to this concrete city where people had hearts of stone. She began to cry as she dragged her little hooves down the street.

She happened to look up and notice a new gallery. Through the window she could see a woman with thick black hair. Darinka liked her at first sight and decided to talk to her about her paintings.

To Darinka's delight, the lady was intrigued by the thought of a little artist deer. She came to the park to see Darinka's work and was thrilled with it. Would Darinka like to have a show at her gallery? Yes, yes, yes! The little deer kicked up her hooves with joy.

The black-haired lady sent a van to pick up the paintings from the park. She also planned a big party for the opening night of the show. Darinka was happy and excited. She hoped that people would like her work, but the more she thought about everyone seeing her pictures, the more nervous and scared she became. Now she was afraid to go to the party, so she crept slowly toward the gallery.

The people at the party were waiting for Darinka. When they saw her coming down the street, they let out cheers and whistles, "Congratulations!" "Bravo Darinka!" "We love you, little deer!"

Darinka couldn't believe it. The crowds parted to let her enter. The black-haired lady rushed to kiss her. Everyone wanted to congratulate her and shake her hoof. They loved her work. The newspaper reporters were there, each vying to be the first to interview her. Cameras flashed. She was a success! Darinka was so happy.

She felt a tap on her shoulder, "I want you to meet someone," said the black-haired lady.

Darinka turned around and could not believe her eyes. There stood a handsome, smiling deer. "Darinka, I would like you to meet Mr. W.T. Deer," said the lady. This was an unexpected surprise at her party!

Almost every painting was sold that night. Darinka was a success not only with the public, but also with W.T. Deer. He was very interested in Darinka. He admired her talent and her courage to come to the big city by herself. W.T. Deer had a similar story to tell. Soon they fell in love and W.T. Deer asked Darinka to marry him.

It wasn't long before the lady with the wonderful black hair received an invitation to their wedding. After Darinka and W.T. Deer were married, the couple went away to the forest for their honeymoon. You can't imagine how excited the herd was to see Darinka and W.T. Deer.

The little deer had become a famous artist in the big concrete city, but the old deer still preferred to lie on the soft grass and rest in the warm sunlight.

A Page from Darinka's Notebook

Must Do:

buy art supplies

phone agent

fax press releases

e-mail friends

manicure - pedicure

Pending:

write autobiography

take dance lessons

sail around the world

save the planet